COUPON #1

STRIP POKER GAME

TERMS:
CAN BE REDEEMED
ONLY ONCE

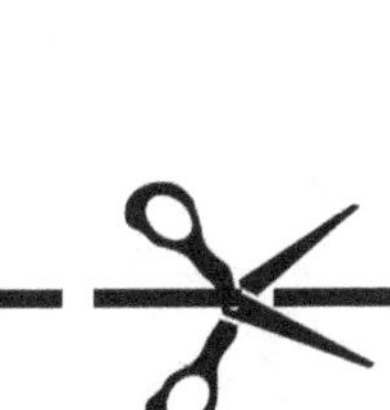

COUPON #2
DESSERT NIGHT
love
TERMS:
CAN BE REDEEMED
ONLY ONCE

COUPON #3
NETFLIX & CHILL
love
TERMS:
CAN BE REDEEMED ONLY ONCE
CINEMA
CINEMA

COUPON #4

SEXY STREPTEASE

TERMS: CAN BE REDEEMED ONLY ONCE

COUPON #5
BREAKFAST IN BED
love
TERMS:
CAN BE REDEEMED ONLY ONCE

COUPON #6
A FULL BODY MASSAGE
love
TERMS:
CAN BE REDEEMED ONLY ONCE

COUPON #7
THE LONGEST KISS EVER
love
TERMS:
CAN BE REDEEMED
ONLY ONCE

COUPON #8
I GRANT YOU
3 WISHES
love
TERMS:
CAN BE REDEEMED
ONLY ONCE

COUPON #9
MASSAGE +
HAPPY ENDING
love
TERMS:
CAN BE REDEEMED
ONLY ONCE

COUPON #10

DIRTY DANCING

TERMS:

CAN BE REDEEMED ONLY ONCE

COUPON #11
NIGHT OF LOVE
love
TERMS:
CAN BE REDEEMED ONLY ONCE

COUPON #12
SEXY DESSERT
love
TERMS:
CAN BE REDEEMED
ONLY ONCE

COUPON #13
ORAL PLEASURE
love
TERMS:
CAN BE REDEEMED ONLY ONCE

COUPON #14
SHOWER FOR TWO
love
TERMS:
CAN BE REDEEMED ONLY ONCE

COUPON #15
QUICKIE
love
TERMS:
CAN BE REDEEMED
ONLY ONCE

COUPON #16
SWEET KISSES
love
TERMS:
CAN BE REDEEMED ONLY ONCE

COUPON #17
SPOIL ME!
TERMS:
CAN BE REDEEMED ONLY ONCE
love

COUPON #18
FREE WISH
TERMS:
CAN BE REDEEMED
ONLY ONCE
love

COUPON #19
WHOLE BODY KISSING
love
TERMS:
CAN BE REDEEMED
ONLY ONCE

COUPON #20

BUY ME
SOMETHING
SEXY

love

TERMS:
CAN BE REDEEMED
ONLY ONCE

COUPON #21
LET'S GO OUT TONIGHT
love
TERMS:
CAN BE REDEEMED ONLY ONCE

COUPON #22
SURPRISE ME
love
TERMS:
CAN BE REDEEMED
ONLY ONCE

COUPON #23
"YES" ALL DAY
love
TERMS:
CAN BE REDEEMED ONLY ONCE

COUPON #24
DISH DUTY
TERMS:
CAN BE REDEEMED
ONLY ONCE
love

COUPON #25
LAST WORD
TERMS:
CAN BE REDEEMED
ONLY ONCE
love